BuSY BuG
Builds a ForT
by David A. Carter

Ready-to-Read

Simon Spotlight

New York   London   Toronto   Sydney   New Delhi

SIMON SPOTLIGHT
An imprint of Simon & Schuster Children's Publishing Division
1230 Avenue of the Americas, New York, New York 10020
This Simon Spotlight edition January 2016
Copyright © 2016 by David A. Carter

SIMON SPOTLIGHT, READY-TO-READ, and colophon are registered trademarks of Simon & Schuster, Inc.
For information about special discounts for bulk purchases, please contact Simon & Schuster Special Sales
at 1-866-506-1949 or business@simonandschuster.com.
The Simon & Schuster Speakers Bureau can bring authors to your live event. For more information or to book
an event contact the Simon & Schuster Speakers Bureau at 1-866-248-3049 or visit our website at www.simonspeakers.com.
Manufactured in the United States of America 1215 LAK
10 9 8 7 6 5 4 3 2 1
Library of Congress Cataloging-in-Publication Data
Names: Carter, David A., author, illustrator.
Title: Busy Bug builds a fort / by David A. Carter.
Description: First edition. | New York : Simon Spotlight, [2016] |
Series: Ready-to-read. Level 1 |
Summary: "Busy Bug has a great idea! He wants to build a fort. But how? Then his friend Bitsy Bee stops by. She shows Busy that there are building things all around!"— Provided by publisher.
Identifiers: LCCN 2015023464| ISBN 9781481440479 (paperback) |
ISBN 9781481440486 (hc) | ISBN 9781481440493 (eBook)
Subjects: | CYAC: Stories in rhyme. | Insects—Fiction. | Bees—Fiction. |
Play—Fiction. | Building—Fiction. | BISAC: JUVENILE FICTION / Readers /
Beginner. | JUVENILE FICTION / Humorous Stories. | JUVENILE FICTION /
Nature & the Natural World / General (see also headings under Animals).
Classification: LCC PZ8.3.C244 Bts 2016 | DDC [E]—dc23
LC record available at http://lccn.loc.gov/2015023464

It is a sunny day
in Bugland!

Busy Bug is at home.
He wonders what
to do today!

He opens the door.
He breathes fresh air.
It is the perfect day
to play.

Busy Bug has an idea.
He thinks it is a good one.

He is going to build a fort.
That will surely be fun!

But how?
Busy does not see
any tools that
look quite right.

"What goes into a fort?"
Busy asks his sister.
He asks his dad.
He thinks with
all his might.

Then there is a knock
at the door.
It is Bitsy Bee!

"Hello, Busy," she says.
"Do you want to
play with me?"

Busy jumps for joy.
He tells Bitsy his idea.
"Oh, I will help you build a
fort," says Bitsy Bee.

The friends go outside.
Bitsy points to a big tree.

"We will build our fort here," says Bitsy. Busy agrees it is the perfect place.

"But what will we use to make our fort?" he asks with a small frown on his face.

Bitsy shows Busy
that there are tools
all around.

A few boxes, a rake,
a bucket, a blanket,
all of these
can be found.

When they are
put together,
they make a fort
that is just right!

The Bugs add a chair,
a few pillows,
and a string of lights.

They find some paper
and some markers.
They make a flag
to mark their spot.

A stick goes into the ground.
Then they tie the flag
with a knot.

Busy Bug and Bitsy Bee
are proud of their
hard work.

They put their
heads together
and built the world's
greatest fort!

Now Busy and Bitsy
share stories
and a snack.
They know that tomorrow
they will come right back!

XINOS